Heather

D0102304

Original
Sylvanian families™

ACORN OAKWOOD
PREPARES FOR WINTER
Jessamy Johnson

FANTAIL

IT was October. The leaves on the trees in the Sylvanian Forest were turning red and gold and there was a chill in the night air, so much so that Betsy Oakwood had already put extra blankets on all the beds in her house. Ollie Oakwood, Betsy's husband, decided that the time had come to prepare for winter.

"BARNABY and Bluebell, I want you to go and collect firewood for the winter while your mother and I store the food," said their father.

Barnaby and Bluebell liked collecting firewood.

"Oh yes, Daddy," they cried. "We'll go down to Copper Beech Wood, there's plenty of wood there." So Barnaby and Bluebell set off with some boxes for the wood.

OLLIE and Betsy Oakwood have two other children. Abbie and Acorn are still very little. Abbie is happy to watch what is going on around him but Acorn always wants to get involved.

"Please may I help Barnaby and Bluebell collect firewood?" Acorn asked her mother.

"Oh Acorn, you're far too little to carry the wood and I don't like you going to Copper Beech Wood in case you get lost," replied Betsy. "Maybe next year when you are a little older."

MEANWHILE, Ollie and Betsy started to pack the food. There were apples and oranges to wipe and arrange in neat piles in boxes, there were potatoes and onions to clean and put in large sacks. Most important of all, there were acorns, conkers, beech nuts, in fact all kinds of nuts, to polish and store in huge jars. Everything you can think of had to be packed away in case it was a very bad winter and the family were snowed in.

OF course, Acorn tried to help her parents. She would try to carry the boxes and baskets for her father but they were much too heavy. She would try to polish the oranges and apples but her hands were so little that she kept on dropping them. Finally, she burst into tears.

"I want to help prepare for winter too," she sobbed to her mother.

SO that Acorn would not get so upset, Betsy Oakwood decided to put out some items that would be safe and easy for Acorn to play with. Betsy chose two empty boxes, Barnaby's best sweater, Ollie's old sun hat and some oranges and apples. She left Acorn playing happily while she and Ollie continued with the packing.

WINTER came and the Oakwood family were invited to Herb Wildwood's famous Christmas party.

"Mummy, where's my best jumper?" asked Barnaby, "I want to wear it to the party but I can't find it anywhere."

"I gave it to Acorn to play with while we were doing the winter packing and, I must say, I have not seen it since." Betsy looked at Acorn who did not say anything.

"Acorn, can you remember what you did with Barnaby's sweater?"

Acorn just smiled at her.

A FEW days later, the snow began to fall. Within a couple of hours, Sylvania had been transformed into a magical, white country. Ollie was well-known as Sylvania's champion snowman builder and this year he surpassed himself. He used two acorns for the eyes, a conker for the nose and orange peel for the mouth. But something was missing.

"Betsy, where is my old sun hat, I want to put it on the snowman."

Betsy looked at Acorn but Acorn still did not say anything.

BLUEBELL then asked her mother for an old box to put some firewood in. But Betsy had given the only two spare boxes she had to Acorn.

"Oh dear," thought Betsy, "I gave all those things to Acorn but she's too little to remember where she put them. It's all my fault."

AT long last, spring came. The snow melted, the trees started to bud, and snowdrops, crocuses and daffodils bloomed throughout the forest. Birds, of different colours, shapes and sizes, flew into Sylvania from all over the world – they liked to spend spring and summer in Sylvania.

All the Sylvanians were overjoyed to put away their heavy winter clothes and feel the sun on their faces again.

ONE fine morning, Betsy Oakwood decided that it was time to tackle her spring cleaning.

"Ollie, I want you to take the children to Copper Beech Wood for a picnic while I get on with my cleaning. Here are some sandwiches for you to eat at lunchtime."

Needless to say, Ollie and the children were delighted. They loved picnics in the forest, whereas none of them liked cleaning. So, off they all set in fine spirits.

ONCE Betsy had waved them off, she got out all her dusters and mops, brooms and brushes, waxes and polishes, and set to work with a very determined air.

"This is going to take all day," grumbled Betsy to herself. But she didn't really mind – Betsy was very proud of her home and liked working in it.

THE Oakwood family owned a particularly beautiful grandfather clock and Betsy was very proud of it.

"I think I'll give the clock an extra special wax," Betsy thought to herself.

Suddenly, Betsy realised that she had not heard the grandfather clock chime all winter.

"HOW very strange," thought Betsy. "I can't remember it ever going wrong before."

Very carefully, she opened the door on the front of the grandfather clock to see if one of the pendulums had broken. Guess what she found?

Baby Acorn, playing at preparing for winter, had stored the two empty boxes, Barnaby's best sweater, Ollie's sun hat and the apples and oranges in the case. No wonder, the clock had not been chiming. And Baby Acorn, being so little, had forgotten all about it.

LATER that afternoon, Ollie and the children returned home with lots of exciting stories for Betsy about their picnic in the forest.

After they had all eaten supper, Betsy told her family how Acorn had prepared for winter.

"I think we had all better keep a closer eye on Acorn next winter," laughed Ollie.

FANTAIL PUBLISHING, AN IMPRINT OF PUFFIN ENTERPRISES

Published by the Penguin Group
27 Wrights Lane, London W8 5TZ, England
Viking Penguin Inc., 40 West 23rd Street, New York, NY 10010, USA
Penguin Books Australia Ltd, Ringwood, Victoria, Australia
Penguin Books Canada Ltd, 2801 John Street, Markham, Ontario,
Canada L3R 1B4
Penguin Books (NZ) Ltd, 182-190 Wairau Road, Auckland 10, New Zealand
Penguin Books Ltd, Registered Offices: Harmondsworth,
Middlesex, England

First published by Fantail Publishing, 1988

Copyright © 1988 Epoch Co LTD
All rights reserved

014 0900039

Made and printed in Great Britain by

William Clowes Limited
Beccles and London